This book belongs to

ISBN 81-7508-375-1

© India Book House Pvt Ltd, 2004

**INDIA BOOK HOUSE PVT LTD**
Mahalaxmi Chambers, 22 Bhulabhai Desai Road, Mumbai 400 026, India
Tel 91 22 2495 3827, Fax 91 22 2493 8406, E-mail publishing@ibhworld.com

# Luv and Kush
## SONS of RAMA

as told by  LAVANYA RAY
illustrated by  VIKY ARYA

INDIA BOOK HOUSE

'Rama! Rama! We're going to be parents, Rama! Oh, how I'm looking forward to caring for my own little child.' Sita was so delighted she danced and sang around her husband.

Rama laughed with joy. 'When the baby is born, every child in my kingdom will feast at the palace,' he promised. 'And all the priests and sages will be invited to bless my heir.'

Rama was the much-loved head of the Ikshvaku clan that ruled Koshala. He had returned to his kingdom after long years of exile in the forest, where he had been sent by a scheming stepmother. Sita had insisted on keeping him company throughout.

Rama adored his beautiful wife. What a shock he'd had when the evil demon Ravana had hauled her, screaming and kicking, to his gleaming city of Lanka, far across the sea. Rama was away, deep in the forest, chasing a golden deer to bring home to Sita as a pet. He had not heard her desperate shouts for help. When he returned home, he found only the flowers from Sita's hair strewn on the floor. Rama realized that something was terribly wrong.

He searched the forest in a frenzy. Where could Sita be? Then, the news came that someone had seen her being forced into a flying chariot. Rama thought his heart would break. How would he find her? He wandered about in the wilderness of the forest so full of sorrow that even the birds and the beasts had tears in their eyes. They gathered around trying to console him.

Hanuman, a monkey warrior, became Rama's devoted friend. He had never met anyone so intelligent, so handsome, and so brave, and he worshipped the very ground Rama walked on. Many people believed that Rama was the human form of Vishnu, the kindest and wisest of all gods in the universe, and Hanuman believed it too.

Meanwhile, in Lanka, Ravana implored Sita to forget Rama. 'Marry me,' he said every day. 'You will live in the greatest of comfort. Your every wish will be granted,' and he presented Sita with yet another priceless jewel.

But Sita would not stop crying. 'Then send me home to Rama. I can only be happy with him. He is my husband.' And she threw away Ravana's gifts.

Rama wandered far and wide seeking news of his wife. Hanuman crossed the sea one day to snoop around Lanka. In a secluded park, he heard a woman crying piteously for Rama. He knew at once that it was Sita, and hurried to Rama with the news.

'I have found her! She is waiting for you!'

Rama immediately organized an army, and charged to Lanka. Ravana's powerful kingdom was destroyed, and Rama himself killed the demon in a fierce duel.

At last Rama and Sita came face to face. 'I thought I would never see you again,' she sobbed.

'Sita,' Rama asked, 'do you still love me?' After all, Ravana was rich and had huge palaces that were always filled with music. Perhaps Sita had fallen in love with him?

But Sita said, 'I'll walk through fire for you, Rama.'

And she did, coming out of the flames unscarred. Rama heaved a sigh of relief. This was proof of love indeed.

Happily, they made the long journey back to Ayodhya, the capital city of the Koshala kingdom.

'They are back! They are back!' A holiday was declared for the homecoming, and everyone dressed in their brightest, most colourful clothes. The people decorated their homes with flowers and rows of lamps, congratulating each other on the safe return of their beloved king.

'Long live King Rama!' they chanted.

Bharata, one of Rama's three brothers, had deputized as king in his absence. He was so relieved to have Rama back that he hugged him over and over again, laughing and crying tears of joy. Running the kingdom had been no easy task! Besides, it was good to have his big brother home again.

Rama soon settled into his own role as king. He worked tirelessly to make Koshala as pleasant as possible for his people. Every citizen, rich or poor, received visits from the king. Was there anything they needed? Were their families well? No wonder Koshala rang with praises of Rama!

As the queen, Sita was always by Rama's side, giving wise counsel. He also welcomed advice and help from his brothers – Bharata, Laxmana, and Shatrughana.

The thoughtful Rama often wondered if he had overlooked anything that may worry his people. 'Have they no complaints?' Rama asked in court one day. 'Speak without fear.'

'Well,' replied the courtier Bhadra, 'some of your subjects believe Queen Sita is making a fool of you. After the joys of Lanka and Ravana's company, she has only returned to you because there was nowhere else she could go.'

'But that is untrue!' cried Rama. 'Sita loves me and has always been a loyal wife.'

'Your people

think that you should turn her out of your home,' the courtier continued. 'The other day, a washerman's wife left him to live at another man's home for a few days. Now the washerman will not let her in his house. "I cannot trust her any more," he says, "I am no Rama."'

Rama was in a quandary. Sita was innocent, but his people had no proof of this. He was torn between his duty as king and his love for Sita. He knew that as king, he and his family had to live by the rules. Sita had to be expelled from the kingdom forever.

It was a very difficult decision, the most painful one that Rama had ever made.

'How will I part from Sita again?' he moaned. 'My life will be so empty

without her. In a few months our child will be born, and I will not be with her. I was so looking forward to being a father.'

But then, determined as always, he brushed aside his grief. He must think only of his duty. 'This is no time for tears,' he scolded himself.

Rama confided in Laxmana. 'I need your help, my faithful brother. Sita has to leave Ayodhya, and must never set foot here again. My subjects think she cheated me and was in love with Ravana. They want her punished. I must send her away.'

Laxmana was horrified. 'I look upon Sita as my own mother,' he cried. 'And I know that she has done no wrong. I cannot help you do this dreadful thing.'

'You must listen to me, Laxmana,' Rama insisted. 'The people will ridicule her if she stays, and they will not have any regard for me either. Do you think that is good for Koshala?'

Laxmana was still not convinced. 'She has always been the perfect wife and queen. What is to become of her?'

'I have thought of something,' said Rama. 'Sita wants to visit the hermitage of Maharishi Valmiki, the famous poet-sage. Will you offer to take her there? The hermitage is not far from the river. Once you cross it, leave Sita, and hurry home without another word.'

'How can I deceive her in this way? And how can I leave her unprotected?'

'The hermitage is nearby, Laxmana,' said Rama. 'Besides, the kind and generous Valmiki will take good care of her. Believe me, if she stays, life may become unbearable for her in Ayodhya.'

And so it was that when Sita became a mother, she was far from the palace of Ayodhya. She was blessed with not one but two babies. They were both boys. Valmiki named the twins Luv and Kush.

Sita often thought of her life with Rama. Valmiki saw how she pined for him, and gently asked her one day, 'Will you come with me to Ayodhya, Sita? I hear Rama misses you greatly. Perhaps he will allow you to come home.'

'No, no, maharishi!' Sita cried. 'If I meet Rama now, I'll only greet him with anger, even though I still love and admire him. I'm upset, but not with him. I understand that he exiled me for the greater good of his kingdom. If only my sons could have grown up with their father…'

Valmiki decided not to urge Sita to return to Ayodhya.

No one, besides the sage and their mother, knew that the infants were heirs to the Koshala crown. The humble hermitage was their home, the surrounding forests their domain. They grew up happy, healthy, and boisterous, always looking for some fun.

Many, many years before the boys were born, Valmiki composed a long poem called the *Ramayana*. A record of Rama's extraordinary life, people still enjoy reading or listening to this poem, centuries after it was first written.

At the hermitage, Valmiki now taught Rama's sons verses from the *Ramayana*. They were quick to learn, fascinated as they were by tales of King Rama's heroism. He had destroyed giants, effortlessly lifted the great bow of the powerful god Shiva, found a way to tame the oceans. Was there anything he could not do?

The boys also learned that Rama had abandoned his wife, Vaidehi.

'The poor woman may still be wandering about in the forest!' cried Luv.

'Unless the animals have made a meal of her already,' said Kush.

'If we find her, we'll look after her,' they decided.

They did not realize that Vaidehi was another name for their mother, Sita.

Valmiki taught Luv and Kush all that little princes should know. They learned the use of weapons, and even memorized all the important prayers and rituals.

'I like our lessons with Maharishi Valmiki,' called out Kush, using his bow and arrow to drop a juicy mango from a tree. 'I wouldn't have been able to reach that mango if he hadn't taught me archery.'

'I enjoy our lessons too,' agreed Luv, patiently teaching his pet parrot a Sanskrit verse. 'But the maharishi doesn't allow us to be lazy, does he?'

Far away in Ayodhya, Rama was very lonely, and often thought of his family. 'Did Sita find her way to the hermitage?' he wondered. 'Did she give birth to a boy or a girl?' He ordered a sculptor to make a statue of Sita in solid gold. This statue often kept him company, a poor substitute for the real thing.

Rama threw himself into making Koshala as perfect a kingdom as possible. Its people enjoyed the comfort that comes from peace and prosperity. As time went by, Rama's priests recommended the Ashvamedha Yagna, a grand ritual conducted by kings to bring greater glory to their realm.

A stately white horse with black ears was chosen for this important event. All the gods were called upon to bless the animal, and a leaf made of gold was attached to its mane. The people of Ayodhya crowded around to admire the splendid horse that was expected to bring them more good fortune. It was led through the city gates by the priests, and then allowed to roam free, away from the kingdom. The king's army followed in its trail.

'Shatrughana, you will be the commanding general,' Rama said to his brother.

As the horse wandered through the lands surrounding Koshala, each ruler was given two options by Shatrughana – fight Rama's army or acknowledge him as emperor. Rama's fame as an invincible warrior had spread far and wide. All the kingdoms meekly joined his expanding empire.

One day, Luv and Kush spotted a handsome white horse grazing under the trees. It had black ears.

'Let's catch it,' said Luv.

But Kush pointed out that the horse had a gold leaf dangling from its mane. 'Anyone who tries to stop this horse will face the wrath of an army. That's what Maharishi Valmiki said when he taught us about Ashvamedha Yagnas.'

'That could be fun,' said Luv. 'You aren't afraid of a little fight, are you Kush?'

The two boys managed to clamber on to the horse's back, but try as they might, they could not make the stubborn animal move an inch, leave alone trot or gallop. Disappointed, they dismounted and tethered the horse with vines to a nearby tree.

Soon, a soldier came looking for the horse, and was startled to see it grazing peacefully, and no longer roaming free. Two boys were standing firmly before it.

'In the name of Rama, the ruler of Koshala, I ask in peace for the return of the horse.' The soldier did not want to bully mere boys.

'We'll fight you for it,' responded Luv and Kush.
'Isn't that what you are supposed to do if someone stops
your horse?'

The soldier slowly took guard with his sword, but he
was no match for the youngsters. Their speed and agility
left him confused. He called for the rest of his troops.

'Kush,' Luv called out loudly, 'I hope none of these soldiers are carrying water. You know how badly it affects me.'

This was a clever trick. Unknown to the Koshala troops, water made Luv swell to an alarming size, and his strength grew proportionately. So, when some soldiers thought they would overpower the boys by dousing them with water from the river, Luv was able to deal with the entire force in a matter of minutes. The brave army was reduced to a foolishly babbling mass.

'I've lost my shoe! How can I march through the forest limping on one foot?' Another wailed, 'My sword! It's broken. I can't fight without my sword!'

'Get these pests away from me!' begged a third. 'They're tearing the hair out of my scalp!'

Shatrughana rushed his chariot into the fray, but Luv and Kush took aim with their arrows and shot the chariot's wheel off its axle. The fierce Shatrughana was sent sprawling. His soldiers fled in panic.

Word of the rout reached the king in Ayodhya. Rama was amazed. 'Who are these boys, so strong and so brave? Laxmana, bring them to me.'

The army reassembled under Laxmana. New weapons were handed to the soldiers, and all the chariots were repaired. Laxmana was set to vanquish the enemy, but at the sight of the children, he stopped short. He found it impossible to be harsh with them.

'They seem such charming boys,' he pondered. 'Let me persuade them to return the horse and leave in peace.' To the children he said, 'Release the horse, boys. I do not want to kill you.'

But Luv laughed in his face. 'You had better guard your own life, old man!'

Kush took aim and shot an arrow that took Laxmana's helmet clean off his head. This annoyed Laxmana, and in the duel that followed, he managed to give Kush a small nick on his arm.

The sight of his brother's blood unleashed Luv's fury. 'I'll kill you, you bully!' he yelled, and sent a hail of arrows towards Laxmana.

How quick the boy was! How tireless his arm! Distracted by his young opponent, Laxmana did not see an arrow heading straight for his leg. The arrow went right through, but it was not a fatal hit.

'Tell Rama!' Laxmana cried, and fell in a faint.

Again the mighty army panicked. Again

news reached Rama that a brother had fallen prey to
two boys. The king was baffled.

'Bharata!' he called. 'Take Hanuman and the monkey force to the forest at once. Those boys need a lesson in humility.'

Luv and Kush saw the monkeys approach and giggled. 'Let's make monkeys of these monkeys,' said Luv.

'The sooner the better,' responded Kush. 'I need my dinner.'

Hanuman thought he would swing rapidly from tree to tree and tire out the boys. But they followed him, quick as monkeys themselves. Bharata charged forward, but before he could get anywhere near, an arrow from Kush's bow dropped him to the ground. Hanuman carried the wounded prince off the battlefield.

'Rama must come himself to save the honour of Koshala,' thought Hanuman, and retraced his steps to Ayodhya.

The king was ready for battle, his

armour and sword by his side. Rama's golden chariot forged a path deep into the forest, and was followed by a force even stronger and better armed than before.

Luv and Kush twanged their bows as Rama approached. Rama had a strange urge to gather them close, to stroke their hair. Pulling himself together, he demanded, 'Where are you boys from? Who are your parents?'

'We live at Maharishi Valmiki's hermitage. We have never known our father, but Sita is our mother,' they replied.

Their innocent words had a strange effect. Rama dropped unconscious without an arrow fired or a sword unsheathed.

'Oh ho! Look at this coward, he's fainted!' The boys danced gleefully around the king.

'Come along, Luv,' said Kush. 'If Rama is such a weakling, defeating his forces will be easy.'

Seeing their beloved leader prone on the grass, the soldiers lost the will to fight. They melted away into the forest. Hanuman, who now knew that the boys were Rama's sons, allowed himself to be overpowered by them. They bound him to a tree not far from the white horse, which was still peacefully grazing.

The horse was lovingly untied, and the golden crown removed from Rama's head. Luv and Kush were thrilled with their booty. 'Mother will like this present,' said Kush, proudly brandishing the crown.

Dirty and hungry, they tramped home to the hermitage. 'Mother, come and see what we've brought you!'

But Sita became strangely distraught at the sight of their trophies. 'Boys, boys! What have you done? Did you kill him?'

'Who? Rama? We don't think so. He took fright at the mere sight of us. Why is he known as the bravest man in the world?'

'Don't be silly. He killed the unconquerable Ravana. No ordinary mortal can do that. Rama has divine strength. Tell me,' asked Sita, 'did he recognize you boys?'

'How could he, mother? We have never met.'

'But we did tell him your name,' offered Kush.

'Lead me to him. We'd better take Maharishi Valmiki as well,' said Sita.

She hurriedly told them the story of their birth. She also explained that they were to bear no grudge against Rama. 'Your father behaved as a selfless king should, even though it caused him great pain and loneliness. I am proud of him.'

'Can you believe it?' Kush asked Luv. 'Vaidehi is our own mother. Now we can always take care of her.'

By this time they had reached poor Hanuman. 'Untie him at once,' ordered Sita. When the boys unravelled the knots, Hanuman fell at Sita's feet, overjoyed to see her again.

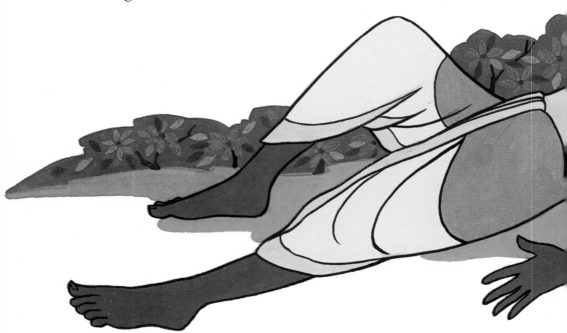

As Rama regained consciousness, he saw his sons peering anxiously down at him. 'He isn't dead, mother,' Luv assured Sita.

The sight of Sita filled Rama with both joy and pain. Before either could speak, Valmiki said, 'Now Rama, you must take Sita home to Ayodhya with you. Take the boys as well. They deserve to live with their father, learning to be great princes.'

'But maharishi,' said Rama sadly, 'having once banished her from my realm, how can I tell my subjects that I have brought my wife back?'

Sita would hear no more. 'I do not want to return to Ayodhya if my husband is ashamed of me,' she said. 'Imagine the humiliation I would face! Now that I have performed my part as a wife and a mother, I have just one wish…' Falling to her knees, she prayed, 'Earth, my mother, if I am innocent, take me into your lap.'

Suddenly the ground shook violently beneath them. Luv and Kush yelled in alarm, 'Move away! There is a crack in the earth beneath your feet, mother. Quick, or you'll fall into it!'

But even as the boys tried to clutch on to their mother, the chasm closed over her. Sita smiled as she disappeared into the ground.

The boys were aghast. Rama wrapped his arms around them. 'Do not grieve, my sons,' he said, gently wiping away their tears. 'They say the earth gave birth to your mother. It seems Sita wanted to go home to her own mother.'

Rama spent the night at the hermitage comforting his children. Before morning dawned, the boys had recited the entire *Ramayana* to their father, from beginning to end.

'You have beautiful voices,' said Rama. 'You are powerful fighters and good at your studies. What else is left for you to learn?'

'We don't know how to ride a horse,' the boys pointed out. 'Will you teach us?'

Valmiki prepared to say goodbye to Luv and Kush. He knew that their place was now with their father. He would miss the boys, but he no longer had any claim to them.

'Do not forget to be always honest and brave,' he warned as the boys touched his feet in farewell.

'And you must not forget us,' they sobbed.

Hanuman led them to Rama's chariot. Soon they were excitedly listening to Rama's account of the uncles, aunts, and cousins that awaited them in their new home, and the names of the horses they could ride.

Ayodhya welcomed the boys with open arms. 'How handsome they are!' said some people. 'Just like their mother.'

'Look at their chins, strong like their father's,' said the others.

Everyone was certain that one day, when Rama was too tired and too old to rule, Luv and Kush would take over the reins of government, leading the kingdom of Koshala to more fame and glory.

## About the Illustrator

Viky Arya is very busy – she is a painter, a
sculptor, a poet, a scriptwriter for films, as
well as the author and illustrator of several
books for children. With a string of awards
to her name, Viky works at a leading
advertising agency as Creative Director.